The
Book
With
No
Pictures

B.J. Novak

PUFFIN

This is a book with no pictures.

It might seem like no fun to have someone read you a book with no pictures.

It probably seems
boring
and
serious.

Except...

Here is how books work:

Everything the words say, the person reading the book *has to say.*

No matter what.

That's the deal.

That's the rule.

So that means...

Even if the words say...

BLORK.

Wait—what?

That doesn't even
mean anything.

BLuuRF.

Wait a second—what?!

This isn't the kind
of book I wanted to
read!

And I have to say
every word the book says?

Uh-oh...

I am a monkey
who taught
myself to read.

Hey! I'm not
a monkey!

And now I am reading you this book with my **monkey mouth** in my **monkey voice.**

That's not true...
I am not a monkey!

Yes, I am

a monkey.

Also, I am a

ROBOT
MONKEY.

WHAT?!

And my head
is made of
**blueberry
pizza.**

Wait a second—

Is this whole book
a trick?

Can I stop reading,
please?

No?!!

And now it's time for me to sing you my favourite song!

A song?

Do I really have to sing a—

♫ glug
glug
glug ♫

my face is a

♫ bug...

♫

I eat ants for ♫
breakfast
right off the
ruuuuuuug!

What?!

This book is ridiculous!

Can I stop reading yet?

No?!?

There are MORE pages?!

I have to read the rest?!?!

My only friend in the whole wide world is a hippo named

BOO BOO BUTT

BooBooButt?!

and also,
the kid I'm reading
this book to is

THE BEST

IN THE HISTORY OF

KID EVER

THE ENTIRE WORLD

Oh, is that so?

and this kid is the
smartest kid
too, because this kid
chose this book
even though it had
no pictures

because kids know
this is the book
that makes grown-ups
have to say
silly things!

and...

make silly sounds like...

GLuURR GA-WOCKO ma GRUMPH-a-doo

AiiEE! AiiEE! AiiEE!!!

BRROOOOoOG
BRROOoOOOG
BRROOOOoOG

OOOOOOOmph!

EEEEEEEmph!

Blaggity-BLaGGITY

GLIBBITY-globbity

globbity-GLIBBITY

BEEP. BOOP.

eeeeeeeeeeeeeeeeeeeeeeeeeeeeeeee
eeeeeeeeeeeeeeeeeeeeeeeeeeeeeeee
eeeeeeeeeeeeeeeeeeeeeeeeeeeeeeee
eeeeeeeeeeeeeeeeeeeeeeeeeeeeeeee
eeeeeeeeeeeeeeeeeeeeeeeeeeeeee

Ba-

DOOONGY

FACE!!!!!

Oh

my

goodness.

Please don't
ever
make me read
this book again!

It is so... **silly!**

In fact, it is completely
and utterly
preposterous!

Next time,

please please please please

please

choose a book with pictures.

Please?

Because this is just too

ridiculous

to read.

The End

BONK.

I didn't want to say that.

B.J. Novak is well known for his work on NBC's Emmy Award–winning comedy series *The Office* as a writer, actor, director, and executive producer. He is also acclaimed for his stand-up comedy, his performances in motion pictures, and his collection of short stories, *One More Thing*. B.J. has brown hair and blue eyes. There are pictures of him, but not in this book.

thebookwithnopictures.com

To the reader
and the future reader

PUFFIN BOOKS

UK | USA | Canada | Ireland | Australia | India | New Zealand | South Africa
Puffin Books is part of the Penguin Random House group of companies whose addresses can be found at
global.penguinrandomhouse.com.
puffinbooks.com

Penguin
Random House
UK

First published in the USA by Dial Books For Young Readers, an imprint of Penguin Group (USA) LLC, 2014
Published in Great Britain by Puffin Books 2014
This edition published 2016

010

Text set in Sentinel, Gotham and Visitor BRK Ten Pro
Printed in China

A CIP catalogue record for this book is available from the British Library

ISBN: 978–0–141–36179–6